THE DYBBUK
IN LOVE

BOOKS BY SONYA TAAFFE

THE DYBBUK
IN LOVE

SONYA TAAFFE

PRIME BOOKS

in memory of Bernice Madinek Glixman
(1923—1997)

THE DYBBUK IN LOVE

And then there are souls, troubled and dark, without a home or a resting place, and these attempt to enter the body of another person, and even these are trying to ascend.
—Tony Kushner, *A Dybbuk or Between Two Worlds*

Sunset through the clouds, air full of ozone and the sweet aftertaste of fallen rain, and she walked home from the bus stop through gleaming, deserted streets, the first time with Brendan.

Side by side all the way back from the library, they had talked quietly, about unimportant things like teaching kindergarten and accounting and the books in Clare's leather-bottomed backpack, while the sky spilled over with rain and the bus' wipers squeaked back and forth across the flooding windshield. Arteries and tributaries of water crawled along along the glass as they moved slowly through traffic, in washes of red and green; the downpour sounded like slow fire kindling everywhere a raindrop hit, matchstrike and conflagration. Against Brendan's knee where it had shed rain all over his khakis, the vast blackboard-colored folds of his umbrella stuck out struts at odd angles: he had offered its shelter to Clare on the library's neoclassical steps, and again when they got down from the bus in the last fading scatter between storm and breaking sun, though she had refused him both times. Now they were crossing a street crowded only with puddles, and Clare looked down between her feet to mark their reflections. No shadows, in this diffuse light; no certainty. Brendan's eyes were whitened blue as old denim, a pale mismatch for the heavy leaves of his hair that he wore drawn back into a fox-colored ponytail; she watched them, and listened carefully to his voice, and prayed to be proven wrong.

The sky had turned a washed-out gold, full of haze, luminous, blinded; unreal as an overexposed photograph, dissolving into a grainy blur of light. Up and down the street, windows that had not been thrown open to the cooling, clearing air were opaque with reflection, blank alabaster slates, like the broken hollows in the asphalt that had filled up and rippled only as Clare and Brendan passed. Rain-slicked still, the gutters and the pavement shone: filmed with light, paved with gold; *goldene medine*. Words she could have bitten from her tongue even for thinking them, because they might so easily not have been hers. *Sheyn vi gold iz zi geven, di grine . . .*

No one's cousin, only child of only children: a spare-boned girl, eyes half a shade lighter than her hazelnut hair hacked short and pushed behind her ears; denim coat that buttoned almost to her knees and a scar across her left eyebrow where a stainless steel ring had been. Her sneakers had worn down to soles flat as ballet slippers, laces mostly unraveled into grit and no-color fuzz. She tilted her head up to Brendan and said back reasonably, "If you think I should be reading Gershon Winkler to half a dozen five-year-olds, you can come in and explain their nightmares to their parents."

His prehistoric umbrella was swung up over his shoulder, cheerful parody of Gene Kelly; she had noticed him in the stacks, rust-tawny hair and suit jackets, before he came up to her this afternoon at the circulation desk and asked why she was always taking out children's books. "I don't see why they'd have nightmares."

"This is why you're the number-cruncher."

For the first time, she saw his mouth warm in a laugh, almost soundless as though he feared someone might interrupt and catch him at it. "Clare," he said, and stopped.

The laughter stayed trapped in small places in his face, the lines around his eyes and the angles of his gingery brows, his lips still crooked slightly to his surprise, her teasing, the conversation that might fork and feather out like crystal into somewhere unexpected. "Clare," he said again, gently. A chill pulsed down her bones. "Will you let me come to you?"

The color of his eyes had not changed, neither their depth nor their focus; his voice was as relaxed and nasal as the first time he had spoken to her in the library. But he was looking through his eyes now, not with them: panes of stonewashed stained glass, and she said, dead-end recognition, "Menachem." Something like ice and brandy sunfished up into her throat, sluice and burn past her heart; she put it from her, as she had weeks ago put away her surprise. Wondering for how long this time, she gave her greeting to this new face. "I was wondering when you'd turn up."

"Constellations follow the Pole Star; I follow you." All his sly chivalry in those words, in this earnest head-cold tenor; her mouth tugged itself traitorously up at the corners, and she wanted to slap Brendan's tender, deadpan face until she jarred him loose. If she could have pulled the long hair and faintly freckled cheekbones aside, stripped down through layers of flesh and facade to the teardrop spirit beneath, she might have done it. But nothing would force him out save a full exorcism, candles and shofar blasts and perhaps not even those, and she did not know a rabbi and a minyan that would not call her crazy. With Brendan's mouth, less an accent than the remembered heft and clamber of another language nudging up underneath this one, he was saying, "There's rain in your hair," and even that spare statement was light and wondering.

She stepped backward, one foot up onto the curb and the other above a grate where a page of draggled newspaper had twisted and stuck. Where the clouds threaded away, the sky was like parchment, backlit; summer twilight would leave this glow lingering below the clouds long after Clare had left Brendan standing in the middle of this rain-glazed street and walked home to her apartment alone, in solitude where no one would surface in a stranger's eyes and speak to her.

"Leave him alone. It's not—do you understand this? It's not fair. To him." Easy enough to tell, once she knew what to look for. Brendan's acquaintance gaze would never track each of her movements with such ardent attention, even her frustration, his inability or refusal to understand that she slammed up against each time: that the world was not made of marionettes and masks, living costumes for a rootless dead man. "To any of them. People always ask me, afterward. They know something happened. So I'm supposed to tell them, *Oh, yeah, a freethinker from the Pale who died of typhus in 1906 just walked through your head, don't mind him . . . ?*" Too absurd a scenario to lay out straight and she clenched her teeth on the knowledge; he kept her smiles like cheating cards up his sleeve. Or perhaps not cheats at all, face-up on the table and nothing at stake but what he had told her, and that might have been worse. "Some comforter you are."

Some things, a century of death and drifting had not worn away. Menachem's wince was a flicker of heat lightning at the back of Brendan's eyes. But he laughed, still with more sound than the accountant, and shrugged; a complicated movement with the umbrella still braced over his shoulder, jounced behind his head like an eclipse. The puddles were drying out from under their feet, mirrors evaporating into the light-soaked air. His voice was less wistful than wry, fading toward farewell. "I'd never seen you in this light before."

She said, more gently than she had thought, "I know. Neither has Brendan. You have to go."

"I would be with you always, if I could. Through grave-dirt, through ashes, through all the angels of Paradise and all the demons of the Other Side, Clare Tcheresky. When I saw you, I knew you for my beloved, the other half of my *neshome*," a quick spill of words in the language that he had given up before he died, in this country of tenements and music halls and tea-rooms, before Clare's great-grandparents had married or even met. ". . . years, I wondered sometimes if this was Gehenna, if I was wrong. The things I have seen, Clare, waiting for you." Brendan's face was distant with the pain of strange memories, atrocities he had never witnessed and laments he had never heard. Within him, Menachem Schuyler, twenty-seven years old and dead for more than three times that, smiled like a snapped bone and said, "You don't need me. But if I could, I would be your comfort. I would cleave to you like God."

Clare closed her eyes, unable to look anymore at his eyes that were not his eyes, his face that was not his face, his borrowed flesh that she would never touch, even in anger, even to comfort. When she opened them again, only Brendan would meet her gaze: denim-eyed, fox-haired, essential and oblivious; already knitting up the gap in their conversation, muscles and tendons forgetting the movements they had not consciously made, the same collage and patches she had seen over and over throughout this long, haunted month. She whispered, before Brendan could hear her, "I know," and did not know if he took the words with him when he disappeared, swifter than an eddy of smoke or the mimicry of a reflection, her dybbuk.

Sunlight fell through the plate-glass windows onto shelves of pale wood, bright covers and spines, and the tune danced like dust motes and photons, *Shtey dir oyf, mayn gelibter, mayn sheyner, un kum dir,* hummed under Clare's breath as she wrapped up paperbacks of Susan Cooper and Laurence Yep for the fair-haired woman who had come in to buy a birthday present for her nine-year-old daughter, an early and voracious reader. Four days through intermittent showers; a half-moon swelling above the skyline for the midpoint of the month. Still Clare stayed too cautious to relax, dreams like an old reel of film run out and flapping in her mind.

Yesterday's rain had left the sky blue as morning glories when she looked up between the buildings, soft with heat: no puddles underfoot to play tricks of light and shadow as she walked from her stop to The Story Corner, and no Brendan by her side. No Menachem today, like a wick sputtering into light behind the woman's lipsticked smile: nothing yet, and that meant nothing.

Always there when she forgot to look for him, until she was looking all the time; courting her with apologies, with history, with fits and starts and fragments of song. *Friling, nem tsu mayn troyer. Oy, dortn, dortn.* Because of him, Clare had read Aleichem and Singer and Ansky at night in her apartment, piecing together the intricacies of past and possession, what might lie on the other side of a mirror and what might kindle up from the embers of a deathbed desire. Like the song she played over and over again, nine-of-hearts piano and Jill Tracy's voice of dry-sliding silk—*and I'm engaged, and I'm enraged, and I'm enchanted with this little bit of magic I've been shown . . .* Sometimes, when she gave him time enough for the loan of lips and tongue to tell a story, he shared tales of Lilith and Ketev Mriri, *mazzikim* like smoke stains and tricksters who could swindle even Ashmedai, even Metatron. The names of his parents, Zvi and Tsippe. His three sisters who had read Shaykevitsh while their brother read Zola in translation. *You are the only living soul who remembers them now.*

Confidences bound to chains between them, a cat's-cradle of need and amazement, amusement and nuisance, and she still should have met him a cemetery. Even a wedding, seven blessings and the glass stamped underfoot like a reminder of every broken thing, would have suited him more than the subway crush of a hot summer's night, coming home from the fireworks: announcements too garbled to make out in the rattle and rush of darkness past the windows and Clare jammed up against an ESL advertisement and a black woman with the face of an aging Persian cat, sure she had lost her mind. But if she had, then so had every second person she had met since the Fourth of July; so had the universe, to let him slip through.

You are why I am here. She tried not to believe him.

Two or three weeks ago, on a day terrible enough to have come right out of one of the picture books The Story Corner sold—alarm that never went off until she had already woken up and yelled at the placid stoplight-red numerals, humid drizzle and buses running late and her coffee slopped all over her hand—he had slid underneath the day's itinerary that Lila Nicoille was reeling off to her, and said something quiet, meaningless, comforting, and for once she thought he and his name were well matched. He could not slide an arm around her shoulders, no brief brush of solidarity from a ghost; but the words were as strong as a handclasp, unasked and given for no more reason than that she needed them. Then Lila had faltered to a halt, her greenish eyes as blurred and surfacing as though she had been shaken awake from dreaming sleep, and Clare felt only cold where she had imagined Menachem's fingers slotted between hers, nothing in her palm but the ashes of another momentary bridge.

No way to explain to Lila, to this woman with sleek blond braids, what about Clare Tcheresky made the world waver like uneasy sleep, déjà vu, like a ghost walking over memories' grave. No way to explain to Brendan, though she had seen him once in the stacks and once walking down the other side of a rush-hour street and his business card lay like a cue on her windowsill at home, why she would not meet him again—give another person's body and soul over to this wandering stranger, to satisfy her curiosity? She could only withdraw, stay alone, and try not wonder too much about what would happen when the school year began. If one of her new class suddenly raised a small head and said in a bird-pipe of a voice, not *Miss T.,* but *Clare*— There were things she thought she would not forgive him for, no matter how lovestruck, how fascinating, and she did not want to find out what they were.

Across the counter, the woman had fallen silent. A glitter moved across her eyes, and Clare snapped her head up, tensing already for the words that would drive him back.

"Is everything all right?"

That was not Menachem's language, nor Menachem looking back in puzzlement and the faintest rim of suspicion: the woman had only blinked. Her eyes were marked out like a leopard's

17

with mascara, even to the tear-line at the inner corners. Like picture frames for her warmly brown irises; like glasses, which Clare did not know if Menachem had worn. Brendan wore contact lenses. Her eyes were going to hell: staring at small print all day, screens and receipts, staring into strangers' eyes. "Yes," she said, clumsy syllable like a weight against her teeth, tongue-twister misunderstanding, and slid the package of books over into the manicured hands.

When the woman had gone, aloud to the gilt-slanting light and the soft white noise of the fan in the back: "Only looking for the truth." Clare pushed her sliding hair back behind her ears; her laugh was little more than a sharpness of air, a puff to blow away ghosts and wishful thinking. *Shtey dir oyf. Extraordinary.*

That night she dreamed of him, once, when the velour air cooled enough for sleep and there were fewer cars honking in the streetlit haze under her window: that she stepped between slender, scarred-black birches into the cemetery where they had not met, and walked among the graves grown up like trees of granite and sawed-off memories, like stumps. Spade-leafed ivy clustered over the weather-blotched stone, delicately rampant tendrils picking through names that the years had all but rubbed out. When Clare pushed leaves aside, scraped softly with a thumbnail at grey-green blooms of lichen, she still could not read who lay beneath her feet; not in this retrograde alphabet, though the dates, in five thousands, were clear. The sky was pewter overcast, pooled dully above the horizon of the trees, and the wind that came through the rustling edges of forest smelled like autumn already turning in cool earth and shortening days.

"Clare," he said behind her, a voice she had never heard, and she turned knowing who she would see.

If anything, she had still expected a character from old photographs and Yiddish literature, a sallow yeshiva student in his scholar's black and white fringes, a prayer for every occasion calligraphed onto his tongue and no more experience of women than the first, promised glimpse of his arranged bride. Bowed over pages so crowded with commentary upon commentary that the candlelight could scarcely find room to dance pale among the flickering letters, nights spent with the smells of burned-down wax and feather ticking, dreaming of angels that climbed up and down ropes of prayer, demons that drifted like an incense of malice down the darkened wind. But he had studied seams and treadles as intently as *Bereshis* or *Vayikra*, taken trains that trailed cinders like an eye-stinging banner and read yellow-backed novels in the tired evenings, and Paradise had not opened for him like a text of immeasurable light when he died, dry-throated and feverish and stranded in a land farther from anything he recognized than even his ancestors had wandered in exile.

He was not tall; he wore a dark overcoat, a grey-striped scarf hanging over his shoulders like an improvised tallis, and wire-rimmed glasses that slid the nowhere light over themselves like a pair of vacant portholes until he reached up and removed them in a gesture like the slight, deliberate tip of a hat: not the movement of a stranger, and it made her smile. Bare-headed, he had wiry hair the color of stained cherrywood, tousled, the same color as his down-slanting brows; all his face gathered forward, bones like promontories and chisel slips. His eyes were no particular color that Clare could discern.

Among the cracked and moss-freckled headstones, he stood quietly and waited for her; he did not look like a dead man, cloudy with light slipping around the edges of whatever otherworld had torn open to let him through, like a shroud-tangled *Totentanz* refugee with black holes for eyes and his heart gone to dust decades ago, and she wondered what she was seeing. Memories patched like old cloth, maybe, self sewed back together with fear and stubbornness and the blind, grappling desire for life. She did not think he was as truthful as a phonograph recording, a daguerreotype in sepia and silver, more like a poem or a painting; slantwise. He might have been thinking the same, for all the care his eyes took over her—puzzling out her accuracy, her details and her blind spots, the flawed mirrors of her eyes from the inside. What did the dreams of the living look like, from the vantage point of the dead?

Then there was half a step between them, though she was not sure which of them had moved: both, or neither, as the cemetery bent and ebbed around them. The trees were a spilling line of ink, camouflage shadows bleeding into the low sky. With his glasses off, he looked dispro-portionately vulnerable, lenses less for sight than defense against whomever might look too closely. If she moved close, gazed into his colorless eyes, past the etched-glass shields of the irises and through the pupils, what she might read in the darkness there . . . "Menachem," she murmured, and his name caught at the back of her throat. So ordinary her voice shook, "Put your glasses back on."

For a moment he had the sweet, dazzled smile of the scholar she had pictured, staggered by the newly met face beneath the veil that he lifted and folded back carefully, making sure this was his bride and no other, and then he laughed. The sound was not seminary laughter.

"Clare, oy—" One stride into the wind that blew her hair up about them, dreamcatcher weave on the overcast air, and she felt him solid in her arms: breastbone against breastbone hard enough to jar her teeth through the buffers of cloth and coat, arms around her shoulders in a flinging afterthought; his delight like a spark flying, the crackling miracle of contact, and she hugged him back. He smelled like sweat, printer's ink and starched cloth, the powdery bark and fluttering leaves of the birch trees that she had walked through to meet him. Desire, wonder, curiosity; Clare roped her arms around his back, her chin in the hollow of his shoulder and his wild hair soft and scratching down the side of her neck, and held him fast. Embracing so tightly there was no way to breathe, no space for air, not even vacuum between them, like two halves of the universe body-slammed together and sealed, cleaving—

The wind rose as though the sky had been wrenched away. Clare shouted as a gust punched into her from behind, invisible boulder growling like something starved and let suddenly off its chain, snapped the scarf from around Menachem's neck and flung it at her throat like a wool garrote and it hurt hard as rope, all the whirlwind tearing at them, tearing loose. Thrown aside hard enough that her shoulder hurt from the deadweight jolt of keeping hold of one of his hands, arms jerked straight like cable and she heard a seam in his coat rip, she watched his face go liquid with terror: whatever a dead soul had to fear from a dream. The headstones were folding forward under the wind, peeling back, papery as dry leaves; names and dates and stars of David blown past her in fragments, bits of marble like a scarring handful of rain, even the flat, plate-silver sky starting to bulge and billow like a liquid surface, a mercury upheaval. When he cried out her name, the sound vanished in a smear of chalk-and-charcoal branches and granite that shed letters like rain. His glasses had evaporated like soap bubbles, not even a circle of dampness left behind. He was sliding away into landscape beneath her fingers.

His eyes were the color of nothing, void, before any word was spoken and any light dawned. When she blinked awake, sweat dried to riverbeds of salt on her naked skin, heart like something caged inside her chest and wanting out, even the close darkness of her bedroom felt bright in comparison. Still she wished she could have held him a moment longer, who had clung to her like a lifeline or a holy book; and she wondered, as she watched the sun melt up through the skyline's cracks and pool like burning honey in the streets below, whether she should have let go first.

Six days gone like flashpaper in the heat as August hurtled toward autumn, and she had seen nothing of him, not in strangers or dreams. The cemetery was there behind her eyes when she submerged into sleep, unclipped grass and birches like a palisade of ghosts, but never Menachem; the dreamscape held no more weight than any other random fire of neurons, brainstem spattering off images while her body tossed and settled under sheets that crumpled to her skin when she woke. She was already beginning to forget his articulate, unfamiliar face, the crispness of his hair and the rhythms of his voice, cadences of another place and time. Once or twice she even caught herself, in The Story Corner's little closet of a bathroom, looking over her reflected shoulder for his movements deep in the mirror's silver-backed skim.

Dream as exorcism, wonder-worker subconscious: it should have been so easy.

Preparing for classes, she sorted away books for the year, old paperwork and child psychologies and mnemonic abecedaries, stacking her library returns next to the Japanese ivy until she could take them back. Air that smelled of sun and cement came in warm drifts through the open windows, propped up permanently now that Clare's air conditioner sat out on the sidewalk between a dented Maytag and ripening trash bags, found art for the garbage collectors; music from some neighbor's stereo system like an argument through the wall, bass beats thumping out of sync with The Verve's melancholy guitars and hanging piano chords, "Weeping Willow" set on loop while she worked. Comfort music, and the smile her mouth moved into surprised her; faded as the phrase's edge turned inward.

Off the top of the nearest pile, she picked up one of the books from the library afternoon with Brendan, considering weight in her hand before she opened it—blue ballpoint underlinings here and there, scrawled notes in the margins, some student's academic graffiti—and read aloud, "*There is heaven and there is earth and there are uncountable worlds throughout the universe but nowhere, anywhere is there a resting place for me.*" It might have been an incantation, save that Menachem did not answer; save that it was not meant for him. Her voice jarred against the rich layers of sound, the dissonant backbeat from next door. Self-consciously, she put the book down, paranoiac's glance around her apartment's shelves and off-white walls as though some observant gaze might be clinging in the corners like dust bunnies or spirits.

Brendan's card was still bleaching on the windowsill, almost two weeks' fine fuzz of dust collected on the stiff paper, black ink slightly raised to her fingertips when she picked it up and the penciled address on the back dented in, to compensate. Swatches of late-morning light, amber diluted through a sieve of clouds, moved over her hands and wrists as she leaned over the straight-backed chair to her laptop; paused the music, *Beside me*, pulled up her e-mail and started to type.

Full evening down over the skyscrapers, a milky orange pollution of light low in the sky like a revenant of sunset, by the time her doorbell buzzed; Brendan looked almost as startled standing in her doorway as she felt opening the door to him, so many days later than it should have been. Out of his suits and ties, grey T-shirt with some university crest and slogan across the chest and a worn-out blue windbreaker instead, he might have passed for one of the students that she had walked past a few hours ago at the library, younger and less seamless, Menachem without his glasses. Some shy welcome handed back and forth between them, too much space between replies, unhandy as an arranged date; he was still smiling, bright strands of hair streaked across his forehead with sweat and four flights of stairs, and Clare gestured him into the apartment with a wave that almost became a handshake, a panoramic introduction instead.

As she stepped past him to lock up the door, deadbolt snap and she always had to bump the door hard with her hip, she caught the odd half-movement he made toward her, slight stoop and lean, arrested: as if he had been expecting something more, an embrace or a kiss, Judas peck on the cheek before she led him in to the sacrifice. But he was no Messiah, anointed in the line of David; there were no terrors and wonders attendant upon him, only halogen and shaded lamplight as he looked absently across her bookshelves, the stacks of CDs glittering on either side of her laptop, back at Clare coming in from the little hallway and she thought her heartbeat was louder than her bare feet on the floor.

Shnirele, perele, gilderne fon, Chasidic tune she had not learned from Menachem, nothing he would ever have chanted and swayed to in his lifetime. She wanted to blame him anyway, as it ran through her head; nonsense accompaniment to her voice raised over the burr of the little fan on the bare-boards floor of her bedroom, behind the door half swung shut and her name in street-vendor's dragon lettering over the lintel. "I didn't see you when I took the books back this afternoon."

"Believe it or not," he answered, "I don't spend that much time at the library. Just that week, really. I needed some statistics." Wary camaraderie, testing whether they could simply pick up where they had left off or whether this was a different conversation altogether, if that mattered, "I guess I just got lucky."

She had to smile at that, at him, dodging any reply

27

as he picked up a paperback of *The Day Jimmy's Boa Ate the Wash* and flipped through the meticulous, ridiculous illustrations. Lights peppered the night outside her window, streetlights and storefront glare and windows flicked to sudden brightness or snapped off to black, binary markers for each private life; sixty-watt eyes opening and closing, as on the wings of the Angel of Death. There was a tightness in her throat that she swallowed, that did not ease. Hands on the chair's slatted back, she observed, "You don't have your umbrella."

Not quite an apology, waiting to see where these lines were leading, "No."

"It was a really scary umbrella."

The same near-silent laugh that she remembered, before Brendan said dryly, "Thank you," and she thought in one burning second that he should have known better than to come here. On her threshold, he should have shied away, not stepped across the scuffed hardwood strip and almost knocked one worn oxford against the nearest milk crate of paperbacks: some twitch of memory, pole stars and shrugging with his arms full of umbrella, should have warned him off.

Never mind that Clare had known no one who had flashbacks from Menachem, leftover remains of possession like an acid trip. She rarely saw again those people whom he had put on and taken off, unless she could not avoid them. Strangers made briefly familiar and not themselves, their secret that she carried and they might never guess: she never dared. If Brendan had any recollection of a dybbuk swimming like smoke in his blood, he should have run from Clare's apartment as though she were fire or radiation, a daughter of Lilith beckoning from beyond his reflection, trawling for his soul. But he was standing next to her desk, perusing children's books in the sticky breeze through the windows, and Clare did not want to know what he remembered from ten days ago, whether he remembered anything; and why he was still here, if he did.

Before she could find out, she called softly, "Brendan," and when he glanced up from Dr. Seuss, no catch in her throat this time, "Menachem Schuyler."

Bewilderment rose in Brendan's face, but no following curiosity. The dybbuk was there instead.

Always before, he had stepped sideways into being when Clare was not looking; now she kept her eyes on Brendan and saw how Menachem moved into him, like a tide, an inhalation, filling him out; rounding into life beneath his skin, his flesh gravid with remembrance. His features did not press up through Brendan's, skull underneath the face's mask of meat, but all its expressions were abruptly his own. She held on to the dog-eared, dreaming memory of his face seen under a tarnished-metal sky, and said quietly, inadequate sound for all of what lay between them, "Hey."

Menachem said, "I dreamed of you."

A sharp, stupid pang closed off her throat for a moment. He had always taken the world for granted, for his own. Half rebuttal, half curiosity, "The dead don't dream."

"The dead have nothing to do *but* dream."

"Don't make me feel sorry for you." Barely six weeks and already she might have known him all her life, to order him around so dryly and familiarly: childhood friends, an old married couple, and her next sentence stopped. Menachem was watching her through frayed-blue eyes, taller in a stranger's bones than she had dreamed him. Brendan stood with *Fox in Socks* in his hand and was not Brendan, and she had made him so. She had always known that there was too little room in the world.

No other way, no reassurance in that knowledge, and she said finally, "I dreamed of you," and shook her head, as though she were the one possessed; nothing loosened, nothing realigned. "He'll never speak to me again," as lightly as though it did not matter at all, another possibility chopped short as starkly as a life by fever and louse-nipped chills; shove friendship under the earth and leave it there, a picture book for a headstone, an umbrella laid like flowers over the grave. "I liked him."

He put down the book that Brendan had picked up, soft slap of hardcover cardboard against desktop, like a fingersnap. His voice was pinched off somewhere in his nose, hushed and sympathetic; no comfort, and perhaps none intended. "I know."

"Our parents never promised us to each other, Menachem," the name like the flick of a rein, the way his gaze pulled instantly to hers, a handful of jumbled letters to make him animate and rapt. "No pact before we were born. There's no rabbinical court in this world that will rule you my destined bridegroom. This isn't Ansky, this isn't even Tony Kushner. I can't write a good ending for this . . ." Too easily, she could recollect the particular scent of him, salt and iron gall and cigarette-paper flakes of bark, as she took a breath that still left her chest tight; barely a flavor in the warm night air, the phantom of a familiar smell. Halfway across the room, Brendan would have smelled like a newer century, Head & Shoulders rather than yellow soap, no chalk smudges on the shoulders of his coat. She said, inconsequentially, "I wasn't sure you'd come."

"You called me." A thousand declarations she had heard from him before, promises as impossible and persistent as his presence; now he said only, "I wouldn't stay away."

Then he smiled, as she had never yet seen Brendan smile and now never would, and added, "I've never seen your apartment before. You have so many books, my sisters would have needed a month to get through them all," and Clare hurt too much to know what for.

"Don't." Cars were honking in the street below her window, hoarse voices raised in argument; maybe shouting would have been simpler than this whisper that backed up in her throat, fell past her lips softer than tears. "I can't look at these faces anymore. I'm trying to imagine what you look like, looking out, but there's nothing to see. You're here; you're not *here*. There's no one I can—find."

His voice was as soft, breath over Brendan's vocal cords; the faint rise of a question waiting to be rebuffed. "But you held me."

"In a dream." She made a small sound, too barbed for a laugh. "Forget everyone else, I can't even keep you out of my head."

He blinked. Faint shadows on the walls changed as he took one step toward her, stopped himself, stranded in the middle of the room away from shelves, desk, doorways, Clare; apart. "I didn't come to you," Menachem said carefully. With great gentleness, no cards on the table, "You came to me."

Clare stared at him. He stared back, Brendan's

eyebrows tilted uncertainly, hesitant. Maybe she should have felt punched in the stomach, floor knocked out from under her feet; but there was no shock, only an empty place opening up where words should have been, blank as rain-blinded glass. Denial was automatic in her mouth, *That can't be true,* but she was not sure that she knew what *true* looked like anymore. He had never lied to her. She had always been waiting for him to try.

Brendan's hand lifted, folded its fingers suddenly closed and his mouth pulled to one side in the wry sketch of a smile; Menachem, she realized, had been reaching to adjust his glasses, a nervous habit more than ninety years too late. "When I'm not ... with you," he started, choosing words as delicately as stepping stones, laying out for a living soul the mechanics of possession, occupancy, that they never discussed, "it's what I said, Clare, it's dreaming. Or it's a nightmare. For a soul to be without a body, without a world ... I don't think I even believed in souls when I was alive," and this shrug she remembered from an afternoon of fading storm-light and streets cobbled with rain. "But I am not alive. And maybe I know better, maybe I know nothing; I know that I was in the place like a snuffed-out candle, where angels take no notice and even demons have better things to do, and you were there. In a graveyard, but there. With me.

"Clare, if there's one thing I want in this world, in any world, it's not to have died—I wanted so much more life, isn't that what all the dead say?" If she should have assented, argued, she had no idea; she listened, and did not look away. "But I would have died an old man before I ever met you. I wonder if that would have made you happier."

Clare smiled a little, though it was not a joke. *Do you love me?* Four words tangible and thorny enough on her tongue that for a moment she thought she had actually asked them, the chill and sting of sweat across her body in the seconds before he answered, and a high school musical flashed through her mind instead. Golde's squawk of disbelief, *Do I what?* and the scathing dismissal of her advisor in college, *took Tevye and made him into a chorus line—tra-la-la-la-la, pogroms ain't that bad!* One of her own great-grandfathers had lost a brother in a maelstrom of shouting students and iron-shod hooves, taken a saber cut across his temple that he carried like a badge through two marriages, past quarantine in Holland and all the way to his New Jersey grave. Those same politics had no more than grazed Menachem, set him alight with ideas, left him for the angel of tenement bedclothes to destroy. Broken branches on the Tree of Life. She wondered if it looked like a birch sometimes.

He was close enough now that if she reached out her arms, she could have held him as in dreams, in the flesh. He had kept the distance between them; she had moved, bare heel down onto the varnished pine as hard as onto folded cloth and something inside that crunched, snapped, would cut if carelessly unwrapped. Menachem was silent, no dares or teasing, cleverness proffered to coax her into laughter, her smiles that had paved the way for him in this alien, unpromised land; quiet, as he had been in rare moments when she saw through more layers than that day's borrowed skin, as he had waited in the cemetery that existed nowhere but the fragile regions of dream. She could send him away now and he would never return, she knew this as though it had been inscribed on the inside of her skin, precise and fiery hand engraving on the level of cells and DNA, deep as belief. She needed no name holier than his own, nothing more mystic than the will not to want; and wherever the soul of Menachem ben Zvi v'Tsippe fled, it would be none of Clare Tcheresky's concern.

She said, knowing it had never been the turning point, this decision made long ago and the dream only its signatory, smoke from the fire that was every soul, "I should never have touched you."

Menachem's cheerful slyness moved over Brendan's lines and freckles, resettled into a twist of sadness around the corners of his smile. Perhaps he had said these words before, perhaps never; no matter. "You still haven't."

This step she could not take back; the glass broken once and for all. "Then come here," Clare said, "come to me." As softly as though the words might summon a storm, make one of them vanish like a drying tear, she sang, "*Dortn vel ikh gebn mayn libshaft tsu dir,*" and turned her hand palm-up.

Brendan's fingers did not close around hers, the dybbuk like an armature within his body, moving him; if he had reached to embrace her, she would have stepped back and screamed like a siren and maybe never stopped. But behind the pupilled lenses of his eyes, a color that was no color swirled, faded, bloomed outward and Brendan fell to his knees, painful double-barreled smack of bone against flooring and she would have reached out to catch him, but nothingness still spilled from him in streams and veils, flesh on flesh too easy a betrayal, and she had only room for one in her arms right now.

Like trying to gather an armful of smoke, over-flowing, reaching out to pull down a cloud: all vision and no weight. No chill against her skin, nothing like body heat, only the steady bleed that she watched disappear when it touched her outstretched arms, her fingers spread wide and her unguarded chest and throat, one skein even drifting against her face so that she saw through it, for less time than it took her to release the breath she had held, into a dull gleam of clouds and pewter, a crumble of ambiguous darkness like soot. Tattered glimpses of what lay between dreams, those of the living and those of the dead, and she would never close her eyes on only one world again. On hands and knees now, Brendan coughed, hoarse and racking, and his body jerked as though all the muscles were climbing away from one another under skin and cotton and nylon; tarantella of sinew and flesh that chattered Clare's teeth, fingers buried in a lightning bolt and not enough sense to pull away, but the last nothing haze was soaking into her hand and gone.

Dimly, through sheetrock and posters, she heard music starting up, the same electronic slam from this afternoon. After all the buildup, what a finish: walking three apartments down the corridor whose doors were all painted the same monotonous sage-green as the banisters and stairs that cored the building, and walking back again without ever asking them to turn down the noise, the endless party that always seemed to be happening behind 5G's door once the sun went down; one ordinary night, with dybbuk. Her head felt no different, if dizzy, her fingers flexed and folded like her own; only someone might have hung lead weights from all her joints when she was not looking, so that she sat down abruptly on the floor beside Brendan, one hand out behind her for balance and the back of her knuckles brushed against the rumpled sleeve of his windbreaker. No danger, now. When she looked over and down at his long, sprawled form, merciful blackout or the next best thing, Clare realized that she was still looking for the little giveaways of gaze and movement and inhabitance, tell-tale pointers to the presence beneath his skin. She had never considered what it might be like to look for them in herself.

She parted her lips to speak Menachem's name, closed them instead. Beside her, Brendan stirred and groaned, "Oh, God," a vague mush of syllables and sense; his face was pressed against her floor, his eyes still shut. Gently, she touched his shoulder and said his name, as odd to the taste as Menachem's might not have been. Still she tried to sort through her thoughts, to find what she would say when he opened his eyes, what comfort or acceptable explanation, this last time with Brendan.

Last few days of the month, as the fragile rind of feather-white moon and the stars she could not see for the city's horizon glow pronounced, coincidence of lunar and Gregorian calendars, and some of the nights had begun to turn cold. Clare had hauled an old quilt from the top shelf of her bedroom closet, periwinkle-blue cloth from her childhood washed down to the color of skimmed milk, and occasionally woke to a sky as wind-scoured and palely electric as autumn. The day before yesterday, she had worked her last shift at The Story Corner, said goodbye to Lila until next summer and turned a small percentage of her paycheck into an Eric Kimmel splurge; some of the stories too old to read to her class in a couple of weeks, most for herself, tradition and innovation wound together as neatly as the braided wax of a candle, an egg-glazed plait of bread.

Cross-legged on her bed, she read two retellings of Hershel Ostropolier aloud to the little pool of lamplight that made slate-colored shadows where the quilt rucked up, yellow and steadier than any dancing flame. She had lit a candle on the windowsill when the sun set, but it had burned down to the bottom of the glass; wax and ashes melted there.

When she leaned over to lay the book down on the jackstraw heap accumulating near the head of her bed, her shadow distorted to follow, sliding bars of dark that teased the corners of her vision, and she made a butterfly shape with her hands against the nearest wall. Out in the other room, *Blood on the*

Tracks had finished and *Highway 61 Revisited* come on, Dylan's voice wailing right beside his harmonica, "Like a Rolling Stone." Homeless, nameless, roving: Clare had never been any of these things, but she knew something of how they felt; and she sang along as best as she could find the melody while she stripped off her clothes, black and white Dresden Dolls T-shirt and cutoff jeans, unremarkable underwear and socks all tossed into the same milk crate in the far corner, and stood for a moment in the lamp's frank shine before turning back the covers. Another chill night, wind like silver foil over the roofs, and she would have welcomed some warmth beside her as she tucked her feet up between the cool sheets; but she had chosen, she might sleep cold for the rest of her life, and she was not sorry.

If she pressed her face into the pillow, she could imagine a scent that did not belong to her own hair and skin, her soap that left an aftertaste of vanilla: slight as a well-handled thought, the slipping tug of reminiscence, a memory or a blessing. *Zichrono liv'rachah.* But her eyes were already losing focus, the Hebrew wandering off in her head toward smudges of free association and waking dream; Clare turned over on her side, arm crooked under the pillow under her head, and said softly into the shadow-streaked air, "*Zise khaloymes.*"

A murmur in her ear that no outsider would ever pick up, lover's tinnitus with the accent of a vanished world, Menachem said back in the same language, "Sweet dreams."

Together they reached out and turned off the light.

My life gets lost inside of you.

—Jill Tracy, "Hour After Hour"

STORY NOTE

Written in August 2004, "The Dybbuk in Love" was a title long before it was a story.

A dybbuk in love, of course, figures eponymously in S. Ansky's 1920 drama The Dybbuk—*the student Chonen, whose spirit possesses the body of his beloved Leah when her father's greed forces them apart and his own obsessive researches into the Kabbalah prove fatal. Not only their tenacious love, but a promise made long before either was born, drives this collision of the supernatural and the commonplace.*

But Chonen died in love with Leah, and as a clinging ghost remains so. What happens when a dybbuk instead, in the course of his rootless wanderings over the earth, falls in love? How do you court someone from inside a borrowed body, when you can never speak to her in your own voice and never touch her except through a stranger's skin? How can she love you back, with that stranger as a sacrifice for every moment you have together? (What if it isn't a stranger at all?) And in a world where dybbuks are as rare as wonder-working rabbis, what does a nice Jewish boy from the turn of the last century have to say to a girl who doesn't even light candles for Shabbes?

Thanks to Shoshana Stern for Hebrew consultation and Michael Zoosman for Menachem. "The Dybbuk in Love" was written primarily to the Klezmatics, especially their 1997 album Possessed—*much of which was originally conceived as incidental music for Tony Kushner's* A Dybbuk or Between Two Worlds—*and Jill Tracy's* Quintessentially Unreal.

ABOUT THE AUTHOR

Sonya Taaffe has a confirmed addiction to folklore, mythology, dead languages, and all the places they intersect. Her short fiction and poetry have appeared in various magazines, including *Not One of Us, Realms of Fantasy, Mythic Delirium, Flytrap, and Say . . . ,* and her poem "Matlacihuatl's Gift" shared first place for the 2003 Rhysling Award. A respectable amount of her work has recently been collected in *Singing Innocence and Experience* and *Postcards from the Province of Hyphens.* She is currently pursuing a Ph.D. in Classics at Yale University.